A Note to Parents and Caregivers:

Read-it! Readers are for children who are just starting on the amazing road to reading. These beautiful books support both the acquisition of reading skills and the love of books.

The PURPLE LEVEL presents basic topics and objects using high frequency words and simple language patterns.

The RED LEVEL presents familiar topics using common words and repeating sentence patterns.

The BLUE LEVEL presents new ideas using a larger vocabulary and varied sentence structure.

The YELLOW LEVEL presents more challenging ideas, a broad vocabulary, and wide variety in sentence structure.

The GREEN LEVEL presents more complex ideas, an extended vocabulary range, and expanded language structures.

The ORANGE LEVEL presents a wide range of ideas and concepts using challenging vocabulary and complex language structures.

When sharing a book with your child, read in short stretches, pausing often to talk about the pictures. Have your child turn the pages and point to the pictures and familiar words. And be sure to reread favorite stories or parts of stories.

There is no right or wrong way to share books with children. Find time to read with your child, and pass on the legacy of literacy.

Adria F. Klein, Ph.D.
Professor Emeritus
California State University
San Bernardino, California

Editor: Christianne Jones
Designer: Lori Bye
Page Production: Michelle Biedscheid
Art Director: Nathan Gassman
The illustrations in this book were created with watercolor and pencil.

Picture Window Books
151 Good Counsel Drive
P.O. Box 669
Mankato, MN 56002-0669
877-845-8392
www.picturewindowbooks.com

Printed in the United States of America in Stevens Point, Wisconsin.
102011
006436R

Library of Congress Cataloging-in-Publication Data
Worsham, Adria F. (Adria Fay), 1947-
Max celebrates Cinco de Mayo / by Adria F. Worsham ; illustrated by Mernie
Gallagher-Cole.
p. cm. — (Read-it! readers. The life of Max)
ISBN 978-1-4048-4759-0 (library binding)
[1. Cinco de Mayo (Mexican holiday)—Fiction. 2. Mexican Americans—Fiction.]
I. Gallagher-Cole, Mernie, ill. II. Title.
PZ7.W887835Maw 2008
[E]—dc22
                              2008006318

Max

Celebrates
Cinco de Mayo

by Adria F. Worsham
illustrated by Mernie Gallagher-Cole

Special thanks to our reading adviser:

Susan Kesselring, M.A., Literacy Educator
Rosemount–Apple Valley–Eagan (Minnesota) School District

PICTURE WINDOW BOOKS
Minneapolis, Minnesota

4

Max and José are good friends.

José invites Max to a special party with his family.

6

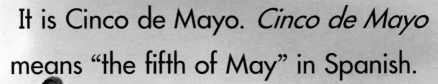

It is Cinco de Mayo. *Cinco de Mayo* means "the fifth of May" in Spanish.

José tells Max that Cinco de Mayo is a holiday in Mexico.

José and his family celebrate Cinco de Mayo in many ways.

11

They have a fiesta. A fiesta is a party.

Max is happy to go to the fiesta
with José.

José and his family make special foods for the fiesta.

They make sweet bread and tacos.

José and his family play music and dance.

Max likes the music and the dancing.

José and his family go to a
Cinco de Mayo parade.

Max goes to the parade, too.

Max and José play with a piñata.

Max laughs when the piñata finally breaks open.

Max had fun at the fiesta.

Max tells José he wants to go to the Cinco de Mayo fiesta every year.